Bitsy the

by Susan Markowitz Meredith

illustrated by Jackie Urbanovic

"Follow me, Bitsy," said Mama Beaver. "There is a lot of work to do."

"I am ready," Bitsy answered. She was always happy to help her mom.

Together they went across the pond.

Bitsy saw a pile of mud and branches at the edge of the pond.

"This is a dam," Mama said. "It helps keep water in our pond."

"Where did it come from?" asked Bitsy.

"Our family built it," Mama said. "But it needs to be fixed." So she went under the water to find some mud.

Mama came back up carrying some mud in her small front feet. She put the mud on the dam.

"I learned something new that our feet do," thought Bitsy. "Our small feet were made for carrying mud."

Later that night, Bitsy watched
Papa Beaver work.

He used his big front teeth to cut down a tree. He bit all around the tree until it fell.

Then, he bit off a branch and carried it to the pond. Papa put the branch on the dam.

"I learned something new that our teeth do," thought Bitsy. "Our teeth were made for cutting down trees."

A noise from the woods made Bitsy and Papa jump.

Right away, Papa lifted his big flat tail.
Then, he slapped it against the water.
It made a loud noise.

The family knew this meant danger. So they went to deep water, where it was safe.

Papa went with Bitsy on his back. He moved his tail up and down to swim fast.

"I learned something new that our tails do," thought Bitsy. "Our tails were made for making loud noises and for swimming fast."

The night turned into day.

Bitsy and her family were ready for bed. So they went to their home.

Bitsy thought of all the things that her body was made to do. She was very proud to be a beaver.